The Big Decision

"Something's got to be done."

Jessica looked up as Ellen and Janet sat down with her and Lila. "About Amy?" she asked.

Janet nodded. "Yeah," she said. "That girl just doesn't know when to quit. We've got to teach her a lesson, and we think we know how. You've got to help us, Jessica."

Jessica hesitated. What if their plan hurt Elizabeth, too? Elizabeth was Amy's friend, and the Unicorns' plan might involve her. Jessica had to be sure Elizabeth would never find out what they were up to.

But whatever the plan was, Jessica was a Unicorn, and she knew she had to go along with what the other Unicorns wanted.

Jessica drew a deep breath. "Okay, what is it?"

SWEET VALLEY TWINS
AND FRIENDS

Choosing Sides

Written by
Jamie Suzanne

Created by
FRANCINE PASCAL

SCHOLASTIC INC.
New York Toronto London Auckland Sydney

Sweet Valley High® and Sweet Valley Twins and Friends®
are registered trademarks of Francine Pascal

Conceived by Francine Pascal

Produced by Daniel Weiss Associates, Inc.
33 West 17th Street, New York, NY 10011

Cover art by James Mathewuse

ISBN 0-590-25006-X

12 11 10 9 8 7 6 5 4 3 2 1   8 9/9 0 1 2 3/0

Printed in the U.S.A.   40

First Scholastic printing, April 1998

Choosing Sides

One

◇

"Where's Jessica, honey?"

Elizabeth Wakefield set the milk pitcher down on the dining-room table and turned to look at her mother. She had a guilty expression on her usually cheerful face.

"Isn't it Jessica's turn to set the table?" Mrs. Wakefield asked.

Elizabeth shrugged. "Well, she's so excited about this cheerleading stuff— She's upstairs practicing. And besides, I'm almost finished with my homework anyway . . ." She trailed off, looking at the table. She knew perfectly well it wasn't the first time she had made excuses for her twin.

Mrs. Wakefield shook her head and wiped her hands on an apron. "Well, go call her for dinner.

It's time to eat, and that means now, not when she feels like it."

"Sure, Mom." Elizabeth tucked a stray lock of golden hair behind one ear and ran lightly up the stairs. She knew her mother's job as an interior designer kept her busy. And that meant Mrs. Wakefield didn't appreciate Jessica's casual attitude about household chores.

Elizabeth tapped on Jessica's door before opening it. As she entered the pink-and-white room, Jessica cheered, "Let's go, Sweet Valley. Let's go!"

"Dinner, Jess," Elizabeth said, leaning against the doorframe.

"Just a minute," her twin replied. Jessica was concentrating on her reflection in the full-length mirror as she waved her arms above her head. Then she executed a perfect stag leap.

Except for the fact that Jessica was wearing a leotard and Elizabeth was wearing her school clothes, Elizabeth could have been looking at herself in the mirror, as she gazed at her sister. They had the same vivid blue-green eyes, long blond hair, pretty, tanned faces, and graceful bodies. They were identical twins, down to the dimples in their left cheeks.

"Jessica," Elizabeth repeated, "this is your big sister calling you back to earth."

"Well, if it's my *big* sister," Jessica teased,

turning finally from the mirror, "I guess I must obey. But who ever said you could be born four minutes before me, huh? I think they got us mixed up in the hospital. I'm really the older one."

"Yeah, right, Jess." Elizabeth laughed, but sometimes she thought those four minutes made all the difference in the world. No matter how identical they were in looks, the twins had very different personalities. That was something Elizabeth had been thinking a lot about lately.

"Seriously, Liz. Do I look like a cheerleader?" Jessica struck a pose in front of her sister, an expectant look on her face.

Elizabeth pressed her lips together and shook her head sadly. Instantly Jessica's look turned to one of panic.

"What? What is it?" She rushed to the mirror again and stared intently at her reflection.

"It's just—oh, forget it." Elizabeth's dimple was showing at the corner of her mouth, but her sister was too concerned with her own face to notice.

"Lizzie!" Jessica wailed, turning her head one way and then the other. She frantically looked over every detail of her image in the mirror. "What's wrong with the way I look? Tell me!"

Unable to torture her sister any more, Elizabeth collapsed in giggles on the bed.

Jessica whirled around. "I'll get you for that!"

she shrieked, hitting her twin with a stuffed animal. For a few frenzied moments, the room was filled with screams of laughter as Elizabeth and Jessica tickled each other to exhaustion.

"Girls!" Their mother's voice drifted up from downstairs.

Elizabeth smoothed her hair guiltily, still giggling. "Come on. Mom is going to kill us!"

The girls quickly ran down the stairs together, both feeling that special closeness that only twins can share. Elizabeth always felt she was lucky to have a twin sister. She thought she and Jessica understood each other better than anybody else ever could.

When they entered the dining room they were greeted by a wolf whistle.

"Who's the babe in the leotard?" the twins' older brother, Steven, joked.

"Ha-ha, Steven," Jessica said, sitting down at the table. "You must be the funniest person in the world. It's such a joy to see you again." She turned to her mother. "Isn't it incredible that the funniest person in the world lives right here in Sweet Valley? And in our house, too!"

Steven grinned at Jessica. "I'm letting you all have the pleasure of my company, so I hope you appreciate it."

Elizabeth sat down next to Jessica and her brother. It amazed Elizabeth how much Steven resembled their father. Like Mr. Wakefield, he was tall, dark, and athletic.

"You know," Jessica began, unfolding her napkin. "Our cheerleading squad is going to make history at school very soon. No one ever thought of having a middle school cheering team before the Unicorns."

"Who's on the team, honey, besides you?" asked Mr. Wakefield.

"Well, Lila Fowler, of course, and Ellen Riteman and Janet Howell. We started it, but Ms. Langberg says we have to have open auditions for four other girls. Which just isn't fair, because it was our idea," Jessica continued, pouting. "But the Boosters are going to be just fantastic, especially since so far we have the most popular girls in the school."

"In your opinion," Mrs. Wakefield said with a smile.

"No, in everybody's opinion," Jessica said. "Everyone wants to be like the Unicorns, because we're beautiful and special. That's why the Boosters are going to be so popular. So far it's all Unicorns."

"Well, I think it's a big joke," said Steven, with a snort. "The sight of you dinky girls jumping around is going to be the riot of the century."

Elizabeth looked down at her plate, suddenly unable to see her sister's new squad as a joke.

Until they had gotten to middle school, she and Jessica had been almost inseparable. They had dressed alike, walked to and from school together, and always done the same things. But since the sixth grade had begun, it had all changed. Jessica was invited to join the Unicorn Club, an exclusive group of snobbish girls, and Elizabeth had started a sixth-grade newspaper.

It had begun to look as though they were moving further and further apart. They had even stopped sharing the room they had grown up in. Elizabeth still felt hurt sometimes when she thought about how much things had changed. Now the Boosters would take Jessica away from her even more.

Mr. Wakefield finished serving and picked up his fork. "When are the auditions?"

"The first round is tomorrow," Jessica said between mouthfuls. "And I can't believe how many girls signed up to try out. We're swamped." She shook her head. "And so many gross girls signed up, it's pathetic. I don't know how I'm going to survive watching them try to do cheers."

Steven laughed again. "You poor thing. What torture!" He held his hands to his throat and gave a strangled gasp.

"Like I said, he's the funniest person in the world." Jessica rolled her eyes in disgust. "I'm serious," she continued. "Girls like Lois Waller,

who's so fat she's really two people, and Leslie
Forsythe—she's skinny and scrawny and always
has a runny nose—and that icky tomboy Amy
Sutton."

"Jessica!" Mrs. Wakefield shook her head and
cast a quick glance at Elizabeth.

Elizabeth remained silent, still looking at her
food. She was remembering the argument she'd
had with Amy when Amy had announced that
she was trying out for the Boosters. Amy was one
of Elizabeth's closest friends. Elizabeth had tried
to tell her that since the Unicorns were running the
tryouts, they weren't going to pick anyone but
their own friends. But Amy wouldn't change her
mind, no matter what Elizabeth said.

"Does Amy think she can get into the Unicorn Club by going out for the Boosters?" Jessica
asked. "If she does, she's got to be crazy."

"Not everyone wants to be a Unicorn, you
known," Elizabeth snapped back hotly. She was
fed up with all this talk about the Unicorns and the
Boosters. She thought they were both ridiculous.
"Maybe she just wants to be a cheerleader."

"Well, that's a joke, because we'll never let
such a tomboy into the Boosters. Cheerleaders are
supposed to be beautiful and graceful. Not like
Amy! She was the biggest klutz in our whole ballet class. Can you imagine her twirling a baton?"

"But she got a lot better, Jess, and you know

it," Elizabeth defended. "She got to dance in the chorus for the recital, anyway."

"Oh, come on," Jessica retorted. "Madame André just pitied her. But she'll never make the Boosters if I have anything to do with it."

Mrs. Wakefield put her napkin down. "Jessica, I'm really surprised at you. The auditions are supposed to be open to everyone. You can't make a judgment before you've seen what Amy can do. Maybe she'll be good."

"Oh, Mom." Jessica squirmed in her seat and flushed uncomfortably.

Elizabeth's face reddened, too. She wished she could stick up for her friend by telling Jessica how much Amy had been practicing—and how good she was at baton-twirling. But Elizabeth had promised to keep it a secret so Amy could surprise the Boosters.

Elizabeth loved her twin so much that it hurt to think of her as cruel in any way. But it seemed that ever since Jessica had joined the Unicorns, Jessica's nasty side came out more and more often.

With a sigh, Elizabeth got up to start clearing the table at the end of the meal. She wondered if she should try again to talk Amy out of auditioning for the Boosters, and decided to call her later that evening.

Jessica finished her milk and cast a sidelong glance at her sister. She knew Elizabeth was upset. But she couldn't understand why Elizabeth didn't realize how important it was for the Boosters to have a good image. Even if Amy Sutton wasn't a klutz, she just wouldn't look right. Her plain face and stringy hair were all wrong for a cheerleader.

Wondering how she could soften her sister's mood, Jessica got up to help clear the table. "Now just what do you think you're doing with that plate, Elizabeth?" she said as she entered the spacious Spanish-tiled kitchen. "Put it down right now or I'll call the dishwashing police. It's my turn to do the dishes."

Elizabeth looked at her in surprise.

"Don't look so shocked, Liz. Come on." Jessica took the plate from her twin. She pouted. "You act like I never do my share, or something."

"I'm sorry, Jessica. I didn't mean it." Elizabeth's mood began to lighten.

Jessica rinsed a plate, speaking above the rush of water. "I know I sometimes ask you to do my jobs for me, but it's only because I'm so busy and I know I can always count on you."

Suddenly all of Elizabeth's misgivings about her twin vanished. How could she think Jessica was anything but sweet and lovable? Jessica might get out of her chores once in a while, but Elizabeth never really minded helping her out.

And for that matter, how could she have

thought that her sister would really be mean to any friend of hers? Maybe her fears for Amy really were as foolish as Amy had insisted. A feeling of guilt for her disloyalty struck Elizabeth's heart, and she watched fondly as her sister left the kitchen.

Just then the phone rang and Elizabeth reached to pick it up.

"Hello? Wakefield residence."

"Jess, it's me." Lila Fowler's snobby voice was unmistakable. Elizabeth started to correct Lila, but was interrupted.

"I've been practicing cheers all afternoon. I'm so excited about tomorrow. But I can't believe how many totally *disgusting* girls have signed up. I can't believe we really have to audition them."

"Lila—"

"How did they even get the nerve to sign up? As if they really think we'd let them in. The Boosters is strictly for Unicorns!"

"But Lila—"

"I know. Don't tell me. Ms. Langberg won't let us do it without open auditions. But you and I have got to think up a way to get rid of these girls."

Elizabeth felt frozen, but managed to say, "Sorry, Lila. This is Elizabeth. Just a minute."

She put the phone down and walked stiffly to the door. "Phone for you, Jessica," she said softly, looking into the dining room.

"Oh, great." Jessica set the dishes she had begun to clear back on the table and rushed past her sister. "Hello? Oh, hi, Lila. Oh, I know. Me too."

Lost in thought, Elizabeth wandered outside to her "thinking seat," a low branch of the big old pine tree in the Wakefields' backyard. She often went there to sort out her problems. Now she was wondering how she could have thought the Unicorns would be fair about anything. Somehow she had to talk Amy out of the auditions tomorrow, or else her friend would be in for a miserable time.

Jessica listened with half her attention as she watched her sister through the window. Her blue-green eyes narrowed and she twisted the phone cord around one finger. She was sure Elizabeth was upset about the Boosters.

"Why does she always have to be that way?" she muttered, feeling guilty and angry at the same time.

"Huh? You mean Ms. Langberg?" Lila sounded puzzled.

"Oh, uh . . ." Jessica's thoughts raced, and she tried to focus on what her friend was saying. "Listen, Lila. If we do it, we can't let anyone know, OK? I don't want anyone to find out."

"Oh, well, don't worry. We'll get rid of those girls, and no one will ever know it wasn't a fair trial."

Two

◇

"I promised Nora we'd walk with her today," Elizabeth told her sister as they prepared to leave the house the following morning.

Pulling on a purple cardigan, Jessica gave one last look into the mirror in the front hall. "OK. Just as long as we aren't late."

"Late?" Her twin laughed. "Since when are you worried about being late to school?"

"Since today's the day we have the tryouts for the Boosters," Jessica said. "And fifteen million wild horses couldn't make me late today."

Still laughing, Elizabeth pushed her twin out the front door. She smiled with appreciation as she looked back at their house. She loved it and thought it was one of the nicest houses on their street. Almost all of the houses in their quiet California town were attractive. Many were far more extravagant than theirs, but for Elizabeth, the Wakefields' split-level ranch had a charm all its own.

Within minutes, Elizabeth and Jessica were in sight of the Mercandy mansion, a Spanish-style house that the local kids used to think was haunted. It wasn't until Nora Mercandy came to Sweet Valley to live with her grandparents that everyone discovered that Mr. Mercandy was really a world-famous magician who was forced to retire because of a stroke.

Nora Mercandy was waiting outside the ornate wrought-iron gate. "Hi, Elizabeth. Hi, Jessica."

"Hi, Nora," Jessica said. "Let's go. We're going to be late." She gradually moved ahead of Nora and Elizabeth in her hurry to get to Sweet Valley Middle School.

"What's with your sister?" Nora asked Elizabeth, nodding in Jessica's direction.

Elizabeth shrugged. "She's helping to run the first round of tryouts today for the new middle school cheerleading squad. She's almost jumping out of her skin, she's so excited—"

Nora laughed. "School's going to be crazy today. The first round of boys' basketball tryouts are this afternoon, too. But if ever there was a born survivor, it has to be your sister! Hey, wait up, Jessica!"

As the three friends approached the school, they saw several groups of girls huddled together like football players. Elizabeth could feel the anticipation in the air. Before she knew what was happening, a swarm of hopeful would-be Boosters engulfed her sister, and Jessica was swept away from Elizabeth and Nora.

Questions were flying right and left, and Jessica didn't know what to do. It seemed everyone wanted to know about the Boosters—the tryouts, the practices, the uniforms. Jessica wanted to answer them, because she was as excited as everyone else. But a quick glance toward the school showed Jessica that Janet, Lila, and the other Unicorns were waiting for her near the entrance. She casually wished everyone "Good Luck" and then rushed off to join her friends.

Elizabeth watched her twin, half-amused and half-sad. "Jessica sure loves attention," she said.

"Well, come on, wouldn't you? Being the center of attention can really make you feel good," Nora said.

"I know, but don't you think it's sort of pathetic? I mean, all those girls think they can get into the Boosters, when truly the Unicorns are only going to pick their friends."

Nora gave her friend a questioning look.

"Come on, Elizabeth. It's not such a big deal."

Elizabeth blushed, afraid she might have seemed jealous of her sister. "It's just that I don't think it's fair to tempt people you don't plan to pick." She watched as Jessica and the other Boosters entered the school. A crowd of potential cheerleaders followed close behind.

Nora sighed. "Oh, well, I guess it's time for homeroom."

For the rest of the day, the level of excitement remained high within the walls of Sweet Valley Middle School. Girls in every class and hallway were speculating about the Booster auditions, and most of the boys were discussing the basketball tryouts.

Elizabeth wished all day that there were some way to avoid the tryouts. But she had already decided to cover both for the school newspaper she had started, so she knew she had to watch.

The gym was already crowded by the time Elizabeth pushed open the heavy double doors. The bleachers were half-filled with students who were there to watch. At one end of the gym were groups of nervous, self-conscious girls in leotards and gym suits.

With a quick glance over the crowd, Elizabeth spied Amy standing alone near the bleachers. She hurried over to have one last word with her friend.

Amy greeted her with a weak smile. "A lot of competition, huh?"

Elizabeth searched Amy's face anxiously, wishing she could find a way to keep her friend from auditioning. "Are you sure you want to go through with this?"

"Elizabeth, come on. How many times do I have to tell you? I really want to be a Booster, and I'm going to try out." She pressed her lips together, and with a rueful smile, added, "I know what you think, but I'm really confident. I know they'll pick me once they see what I can do. But thanks anyway. I know you're only trying to help." With that she walked away.

Taking a seat on the bleachers, Elizabeth watched anxiously hoping that in the face of so much competition, Amy would just call it quits and walk away. That way she would save herself from whatever trick the Unicorns had in store for her and the others.

As Elizabeth sat, worrying and wondering, her sister, Lila, Ellen, and Janet came out of the locker room, dressed in identical purple leotards and white tights. And they all had identical expressions on their faces—regal, and bored.

"Okay, everybody. Get in a line, or something, all right?" Lila Fowler, with a clipboard in one hand and a pencil in the other, was in charge. Standing with one hip out, and casting cold, intimidating glances at the line of girls, Lila was both impressive and frightening.

She casually flipped her luxurious, light-brown hair back over one shoulder and looked several girls over from head to toe and then made some light check marks on her clipboard. Her cold scrutiny obviously did the trick, because several girls meekly stepped away from the line, mumbling excuses and hurrying for the locker room.

Finally she spoke. "Today we're going to teach you one cheer, and you have to perfect it for the final auditions next week. Anybody who doesn't get it right will be out, OK? Jessica, go ahead."

Elizabeth watched with a fresh feeling of anxiety as her sister stepped forward. Jessica's attitude and expression made her almost a stranger to Elizabeth. She couldn't believe her own twin could act so superior.

"Now," Jessica began, with her hands on her hips, "let's take a boy's name, like . . . Tom, for example. Okay, here's the cheer." She began the routine, her long, slim legs and arms flashing energetically as she chanted, "Tom, Tom, he's our man! If he can't do it, no one can!" Her voice echoed throughout the gymnasium, and she ended with a triumphant leap.

Elizabeth could tell by the expressions of some of the girls that her sister had inspired them with her graceful movements, clear voice, and air of confidence. Elizabeth knew her sister loved the attention.

"OK, I'll go through it again, and this time, follow what I do."

With renewed energy, Jessica began the cheer for a second time, but slower. The ragged line of girls before her tried bravely to keep up with the leg and arm movements. Very few of them even attempted to coordinate the words with the motions. Giggles, blushes, and angry self-criticism were evident, and Jessica gloated inwardly, confident that most would drop out from sheer embarrassment.

Finally Lila stepped forward and quieted the group with her haughty voice. "Now, break up into groups of five. First group, step forward, and we'll do some baton drills. The rest of you practice the cheer." She and Jessica exchanged smiles. No one could accuse them of unfair auditions if all the girls trying out were about as uncoordinated as rhinoceroses.

Amy and four other girls moved shyly away from the rest. "We'll go first," one of them said.

"All right, here are five batons," Ellen said with a toss of her dark curls as she handed them out. "I'm going to show you how to twirl them. And believe me, it isn't easy."

Ellen's deep-blue eyes narrowed in concentration as she twirled her baton skillfully between the fingers of her right hand. Then with a flourish, she tossed it up, caught it, and bowed, a smile lighting her dark-blue eyes.

"Now I'll do it in slow motion, and you try it."

As Ellen went through the process step-by-step, Elizabeth looked up from the rough draft of her article and saw with a start that Amy was now in the middle of the baton drills. But to her surprise, Amy seemed to be pretending she was just learning. Her forehead was creased as she slowly—and clumsily—rolled that baton over her fingers.

Elizabeth tried to read her friend's expression. Why wasn't she showing them what she could do? If Amy wanted so badly to be a Booster, she should run through her whole baton routine. It suddenly occurred to Elizabeth that maybe she had changed her mind. Maybe she was just waiting to make a quiet exit with the rest of the girls who were dropping out. Elizabeth closed her eyes with relief.

Standing apart from Ellen and her pupils, Jessica, Lila, and Janet watched critically. "What a bunch of dorks," Jessica whispered to Lila.

Jessica's gaze came to rest on Amy Sutton, who was trying just as awkwardly as the others to master her first routine. As if she felt Jessica's eyes on her, Amy looked up from her baton and dropped it with a clatter. Red-faced, Amy bent over to pick it up. Her limp hair fell in her face.

With an inward sigh of relief, Jessica shook her head. *Well, that's that,* she thought to herself. *Amy Sutton's such a klutz that even Elizabeth won't think it's unfair when we tell her to get lost!*

Three

◇

Elizabeth sat on the bleachers, looking at the notes for her article. She figured it would be more interesting to tie the two tryouts together. With that in mind, she glanced back and forth between the two halves of the gym, collecting material for her story.

On one side, many girls were still stumbling through the cheer, laughing at themselves, and trying to look good, all at the same time. Several of them were pretty good, but many of them were not, and they knew it.

Across the room, the gym floor seemed to be crowded with boys. They were yelling and whistling, shooting baskets and dribbling in tight circles. The air was filled with the sharp squeaks of sneakers on the waxed floor and the pounding thud of basketballs.

Elizabeth noticed the locker-room door on the boys' side of the gym swing open slowly. Ken Matthews stepped out and paused, as if unsure whether to go any farther. He walked hesitantly into the noisy gym and stopped by the bleachers just a few steps in front of Elizabeth, then looked around.

Elizabeth glanced curiously from him to the other boys. Something seemed to be holding Ken back, and she wasn't sure what it was. Just then, Bruce Patman, a seventh grader who Elizabeth thought was obnoxious, turned and spotted Ken near the bleachers. With a grin on his face, Bruce yelled out, "Hey, midget!"

A chorus of other boys took up the jeer. Blushing furiously, Ken turned to leave the gym. He walked past Elizabeth, tripped over her book bag, and banged his shin on the lowest step of the bleachers.

"Oh, Ken! I'm so sorry."

He looked up into her face. "Oh, uh, it's OK," he mumbled.

Elizabeth quickly pulled her book bag out of the way. "Boy, I could really kill someone that way," she said with a smile.

"No problem." Ken started heading for the locker room.

"Hey, Ken?" Elizabeth looked at him curiously.

He paused, glancing nervously from Elizabeth to the door. She stood up and walked toward him.

"You aren't leaving, are you? Aren't you trying out for the team?"

"I'm done," Ken said.

"Done? But they haven't even started yet." Elizabeth looked at him more closely. He seemed very nervous and kept looking over at the crowd of boys. He turned back to her, blushing.

"Look at those guys," he said, jerking a thumb over his shoulder.

"What about them?" Elizabeth asked as she looked over the basketball court.

Ken folded his arms, embarrassment turning his face red. "Well . . . they're all so much taller than I! I'll never make the team. I'm the shortest guy in the whole school."

It was true. Elizabeth tried not to smile. Even she was taller than Ken.

"You probably think that's dumb, but it isn't!" Ken turned away again, looking hurt and embarrassed.

Stricken with compassion, Elizabeth said, "Ken, come on. I know what you mean. But so what? You don't have to be a giant to be a good basketball player."

"Let's face it, Elizabeth. Nobody's going to pick me when there are guys like Bruce Patman and Tim Davis to choose from." Ken kicked his foot angrily against the bleachers.

"Listen, Ken. So what if you're shorter than they are? I don't see why you don't try out if that's what you really want."

He shrugged. "I don't know. Maybe I don't really want to join the stupid old basketball team anyway."

"Then why did you come this far?" Elizabeth challenged. "Are you sure you don't want to join this stupid old team?"

Shaking his head, Ken grinned. "You're right, Elizabeth. I do want to." He looked over at the other boys again. "It's just that—well, they're always making fun of me because I'm so short." He paused uncomfortably. "They call me midget. That's not so easy to take, you know?"

Elizabeth glanced over at Bruce Patman. Just because he was from one of the richest families in Sweet Valley, it didn't give him the right to tease anyone he wanted. "Well, how would you like it if you were called 'Blondie' all the time? Bruce Patman used to call me and Jessica that. He still does sometimes, because he thinks it's so funny. But who cares what he thinks? I sure don't."

She took Ken's arm and shook it gently. "Go on, Ken. Just try your best and forget about them."

Ken looked at Elizabeth's warm, open face and smiled. "OK. I'll go for it."

"All right, Ken!" With a sigh, Elizabeth watched him square his shoulders and walk onto the basketball court.

At that moment, Coach Cassels came out of the locker room with a clipboard in one hand and a whistle in the other. *"All right!"* he yelled after a shrill whistle blast. "Let's have a lineup *now!"*

A frenzied scurry followed, with all the boys trying to get in the lineup at the same time. Ken tried to find a place somewhere in the middle, but he was butted out a couple of times. He finally stood at the far end of the line.

"All right! Now, let's see here." Coach Cassels rubbed his hand over his crew cut and looked down the list on his clipboard. "Looks like we have a couple of familiar names here. We've got a Patman, I see."

Bruce grinned widely.

"And aha! We've got Ken Matthews!"

At the end of the line, Ken went suddenly rigid.

The coach held his clipboard by his side, and with a reminiscent look on his face, said, "Boys, I hope you all realize who Ken Matthews's father is." He shook his head, smiling. "Scott Matthews was one of my all-time great players. Why, there were some games where he did everything. He was offense, he made the lay-ups, the foul shots—

basically all the scoring. Took us all the way to the All-State Championships.

"And handle the ball? You never saw such handwork. He was all over the place with a basketball. And"—he pointed a finger at the line in front of him—"he almost never fouled out. He was always a real gentleman on the court, and very graceful for such a tall guy."

A couple of boys giggled, nudging each other and nodding toward Ken.

"Now, I'm not saying you should all be like him. I'm not saying you've all got to live up to the reputation of one of the greatest ball players in Sweet Valley history. No, I'm not saying that at all."

With a happy grin on his face, the coach walked forward and clapped his hand on the shoulder of Tim Davis, the tallest boy in the lineup. "No. As long as we've got Ken here, it'll be smooth sailing all the way."

There was shocked silence. Then a huge guffaw escaped from Bruce Patman. "Hey, coach! That's not Matthews! Matthews is the midget at the end of the line!"

Coach Cassels looked down the line to where Ken stood blushing, a look of confusion on his face. "You mean . . .?" He held his hand on the shoulder of Tim Davis, as if he were still sure Tim was Ken Matthews.

"I'm Ken Matthews," Ken nearly whispered.

Coach Cassels collected himself and smiled broadly as he walked over to Ken. "Well, son, sorry for the mix-up. I didn't know you'd be so . . . Well, I bet you inherited your dad's shooting arm, eh?"

Ken cleared his throat nervously. "I don't know, sir."

"Well, let's come over here and see what you can do."

Striding forward, the coach picked up a basketball and bounced it to Ken. But Ken was so nervous that he fumbled the ball and had to chase it halfway across the gym.

"That's all right, Ken. Let's see you shoot now." The coach was beginning to look uncomfortable.

"Yeah, midget, let's see that old Matthews arm in action." Bruce Patman never seemed to tire of teasing Ken, and Ken never heard Bruce's jeering voice without the same sinking sensation in his stomach.

"Let's have none of that, now," the coach said sternly. "Come on, Ken. Let's have a couple from the foul line."

Ken's forehead was creased with concentration. He wanted so much to show up Bruce and the others. He bounced the ball a few times and let it fly for the basket, but he wasn't surprised that the ball didn't go in. Amid taunts from the boys and the coach's urgings, he tried a couple more shots. They were even worse.

"I don't think I've got my dad's arm," Ken mumbled, as he dropped the ball again. "Why don't you let someone else shoot?"

"No problem," said the coach in a hearty voice. "But don't give up yet, son. I bet you're a great ball handler. Here, let's see if you can steal it away from me."

With a stricken look on his face, Ken made a few half-hearted attempts to grab the ball away from Coach Cassels. But the coach eluded him every time.

Finally, the coach stopped and blew a short blast on his whistle. "Okay, you guys. Everyone get a ball and do some lay-ups for a minute." Then, turning to Ken, he continued in a low tone. "Listen, son, I can understand it if you're nervous. I guess I probably put you on the spot a little too much there, so I'll tell you what I'm going to do."

From the bleachers, Elizabeth could see Ken deep in conversation with Coach Cassels. She smiled to think they were getting along so well. She gathered her books together and walked over to where the cheerleading group was getting ready to break up.

Ken noticed her leave and stared at the floor, trying to focus on what the coach was saying.

"For your dad's sake, Ken, I'm willing to give you a chance, let you take a few days to work on your shooting, you know."

Ken nodded.

The coach rubbed his chin. "But I've got to tell you, son, if you don't improve a little, I'm afraid even my feelings for your father won't get you on this team. There are a lot of good players trying out, and it wouldn't be fair to them."

"I know, coach. I understand." Ken continued to stare at the floor.

With a sad smile, the coach ruffled Ken's hair. "OK, let's get out there and practice, OK? Just relax. Loosen up. You'll do fine."

Four

◇

Elizabeth gathered up her books and walked over to Amy. Lila had declared the tryouts officially over, but there were plenty of girls hanging around, talking, and some were still practicing. "Amy, do you want to walk home with me?" Elizabeth asked. "There are some stories for the paper I want to talk about."

Amy brushed her straw-colored hair out of her eyes and looked absently at Elizabeth. "Uh . . . no thanks, Elizabeth. I'm going to stay here for a while and work on this cheer."

With a thin smile, Elizabeth nodded. "Sure. I understand. I'll talk to you tomorrow, okay?"

"Sure." Amy was concentrating again, and barely looked up.

Elizabeth stayed for a moment, looking at her

friend. Finally, she collected herself and looked around for her sister.

Jessica was sitting on the bleachers with Lila and Ellen, laughing at some joke. Elizabeth knew the three girls thought of themselves as glamorous and popular because they were members of the Unicorn Club. But Elizabeth thought the Unicorn Club was silly. She wished Jessica didn't spend so much time with them. She squared her shoulders and walked forward.

"Hi, Jessica. Are you ready to go home?"

Still laughing, Jessica looked down at her sister her smile quickly disappearing. "Oh, Lizzie, I forgot to tell you. I'm going to the Dairi Burger with Lila. You don't mind, do you?"

Elizabeth forced a smile. "No problem. I'll see you at home." She turned to go.

"Lizzie?"

Glancing over her shoulder, Elizabeth saw her twin looking at her.

"Weren't the tryouts great?" Jessica said enthusiastically.

Elizabeth nodded and smiled sadly. "Sure, Jess. They were great. Bye, Lila. Bye, Ellen."

"Goodbye, Elizabeth."

All the way to the gym doors, Elizabeth walked with her usual confident stride. But once she was through and alone in the hallway, she stopped and leaned against the row of lockers.

She felt completely alone. Both Amy and Jessica were more interested in the Boosters than they were in her.

Elizabeth stayed there for a few moments, and then, still feeling sorry for herself, pushed herself away from the wall and strolled down the corridor.

Ahead of her, the door to the boys' locker room opened, and Ken Matthews slowly walked out, his gym bag slung over one shoulder, his head down. Elizabeth looked at him for a moment, wondering how the tryouts had gone. She decided to catch up with him.

"Hey, Ken! Wait up."

Ken didn't seem to hear her.

"Ken? Ken! Wait up!" Elizabeth swung her own book bag over her shoulder and jogged down the hallway after him. Breathless, she caught up with him. "Ken, didn't you hear me?"

She turned him around to face her. With a sinking sensation in her stomach, Elizabeth realized he had been crying. Without a word, she fell into step beside him.

Just then, the door behind them reopened, and Bruce Patman and a horde of his friends surged into the corridor.

"Hey, midget!" yelled Bruce. "Maybe instead of trying out for the team you should try out for being the basketball."

Bruce and his buddies shrieked and hooted with laughter as they left through another door. Ken simply lowered his head farther and increased his pace.

Shaking her head in disgust, Elizabeth cast a sidelong glance at Ken. "Ignore them, Ken. Only jerks make fun of other people."

But Ken pulled his head back angrily at that. "But they're right!" he choked. "I'm too short, and I can't do it at all. I'll never make the team." He pressed his lips together as he looked back toward the gym. "I was a joke in there."

Elizabeth suddenly realized how unhappy and disappointed Ken must be, and she felt a wave of sympathy for him. She could never stand to see anyone upset.

"Hey, listen, Ken. My brother, Steven, is on the junior varsity team at Sweet Valley High. Maybe he can give you some pointers." She looked hopefully into Ken's downcast face.

He shrugged.

"Come on," Elizabeth continued. "Why don't you come home with me? He's really good, and I bet he could show you some drills or something that you could work on."

Ken shrugged again. "Why should he? Why should I, anyway?"

Elizabeth's turquoise eyes narrowed. "Look,

Ken. You can't tell me you don't still want to make the team. I think you should give it another shot before you give up."

Ken met Elizabeth's gaze, a glimmer of hope in his eyes. He drew a deep breath. "Do you really think he could help?"

A wide grin broke over Elizabeth's features. "Sure. I'm sure he can. Let's go!"

On the way home, Elizabeth and Ken talked about Sweet Valley and about their families. Finally, Ken told Elizabeth how much he admired his father.

"He was such a hero, you know?" he said. His eyes lit up with pride. "That's why I want to make the team. I mean, I know I'll never be as good as him, but if I get on, maybe he'll be proud of me."

Elizabeth looked at him and shifted her book bag to the other hand. "I'm sure your dad's proud of you anyway, Ken."

Ken kicked at a stone and blushed. "Thanks, Elizabeth." He glanced at her quickly and then looked away. "But this would make him, I don't know . . ."

With a soft smile, Elizabeth said, "I know what you mean."

Ken smiled again. "Well, anyway. No more dumb talk about me. Is this your house?" he asked as they arrived at the Wakefields.' "It's really nice."

Elizabeth loved to hear people admire her family's house. "Thanks," she answered, opening the door. "Want something to eat? I'm not sure if Steven is home yet."

"Sure. Thanks," Ken said as they entered the spacious, sunny kitchen.

Elizabeth and Ken were eating peanut-butter-and-jelly sandwiches when Steven burst into the room.

He yanked open the refrigerator door and stood glaring at its contents. "Isn't there anything to eat?" he muttered, running a hand through his wavy dark hair.

"Uh, I think there's a jar of mayonnaise, and that's about it," Elizabeth teased, winking at Ken.

Ken smiled back nervously. Elizabeth could see Ken's uncertainty as he eyed her growling brother.

"Cute, Elizabeth. That'll go real good with this stuff." Steven was piling bologna, ham, lettuce, milk, and cheese into his arms, and holding the towering heap steady with his chin. He stuck a jar of mayonnaise under his arm as he frantically scanned the crowded refrigerator again. "Don't tell me we don't have any bread."

"Relax, Steven. It's over on the counter." Elizabeth glanced at Ken as her brother began constructing one of his tremendous after-school sandwiches. "Hey, Steven, this is Ken Matthews."

"Hi," Steven grunted, not looking up from the counter.

Ken began to stand. "Uh, maybe I'd better go, Elizabeth. Thanks for the sandwich." He was remembering how Bruce and the others had taunted him, and didn't think he could take any more.

"No. Hey, Ken, stay. Okay?" Elizabeth pleaded. She pushed her chair back and walked over to where her brother stood, eating his sandwich. She pulled nervously at her ponytail, then threw it back over her shoulder.

"Steven? Ken is trying out for the basketball team, and I thought maybe you could give him a few pointers. . . ." She trailed off, looking into her brother's face.

Steven looked at her and then at Ken. He gulped down most of his glass of milk, then looked at Elizabeth again. "Okay," he said, wiping his mouth with the back of his hand. "But just for a while."

"Oh, great!" Elizabeth exclaimed. But Ken looked even more alarmed than he had when Steven first came in.

"OK, now let's see you shoot," Steven began when they were outside. "You know how to shoot, don't you?" With a skeptical look at Ken, Steven bounced the basketball toward him.

Ken gulped. He was determined not to tense up the way he had in front of Coach Cassels.

"Go on, Ken." Elizabeth sensed his nervousness and gave him a reassuring nod.

"Here goes," Ken mumbled. He bounced the basketball a couple of times, and then, squeezing his eyes shut, hurled it toward the basket.

With a dull thud and a twangy vibration, the ball rebounded heavily off the rim of the basket. Steven caught it neatly in one hand and bounced it back to Ken. "Try again."

Ken aimed the ball and made another futile attempt.

Steven sniffed and cleared his throat, his brown eyes showing more than a trace of impatience. "Look, how about we work on moving the ball, you know, passing and stuff?" He shot a look at Elizabeth that made it clear that he was only putting up with this for her sake.

"Sure," Ken agreed hastily. "Whatever you say."

For the next fifteen minutes, Elizabeth and Steven tried their best to help Ken with dribbling and passing, but they spent most of the time chasing the ball after Ken had dropped it.

Breathless, Elizabeth ran back to the driveway with the ball. "All right, let's go again."

"Listen, Ken. I think I've finally figured out what your problem is," Steven said, scratching his head. "I think you close your eyes all the time. Keep them on the ball, you know? Watch it when you've got it and when you pass it. Never let it out of your sight, all right? That way you always know where it's going."

"OK, sure. Keep my eyes on the ball." Ken nodded eagerly.

Steven rolled his eyes and drew a deep breath. "Let's try it again, OK? And watch the ball."

But after a few more minutes, Steven had had enough. "Hey, Liz," he said, jamming his hands in the pockets of his jeans. "I've got to go get some homework done." He looked pityingly at Ken. "Just keep it up. Good luck."

"Thanks." Ken watched as Steven ran back into the house. All of his hopes were crushed.

He turned back to Elizabeth, shaking his head. "I guess I'm pretty bad, huh?" he said with a weak laugh. "Thanks for trying to help, though." He swallowed hard as he picked up his books and turned to leave.

Elizabeth watched Ken walk slowly down the driveway, unable to find the right words to bring him back. She fought back a choking sensation in her throat, and her thoughts went back to all the times she and Jessica had practiced together and what fun they'd had.

"*Ken*! Hey, wait! I just thought of something! It's an unbeatable trick!" Elizabeth sprinted down the driveway and caught up with Ken. He swung around to face her.

"What?" He looked at her curiously.

Catching her breath, Elizabeth led him back up to the house. "When we were little Jessica and I used to play basketball with a tennis ball, because Steven was always such a hog with the basketball." She pushed a stray lock of hair behind one ear, eagerly explaining their game. "And it's really good practice, because the ball is so small. It really makes you concentrate. Wait here a second."

She dashed into the garage and found a tennis ball, and raced back out to where Ken was standing. He had a look of surprise on his face.

"OK, just do this," she said, slowly and carefully bouncing the tennis ball in the driveway. "See? And you can even practice bouncing it behind you and stuff, because it's so small it doesn't get in your way."

With mounting excitement, Ken watched Elizabeth dribble the tennis ball. He could see what she meant.

"Here, let me try," he said, holding out his hand.

Elizabeth laughed with relief. "Here, take this one. I'll find another."

Soon both of them were bouncing tennis balls, concentrating on the drill. Ken found he could handle the smaller ball more easily, and he began to think it might actually help when he tried with the basketball again.

With a burst of confidence, Ken made a shot for the basket. To his great amazement, the tennis ball sailed cleanly through the net.

He looked at Elizabeth with an expression of sheer amazement on his face. But he quickly turned serious. "Listen, Elizabeth? Could you do me a favor?"

Elizabeth looked over at him, her eyebrows raised. "Sure. What is it?"

"Do you think you could keep this all a secret? I mean, I don't want anybody to know you and Steven were helping me, OK?"

"Is that all?" Elizabeth grinned and made a shot for the basket. "No problem, Ken. All right!" she yelled as her ball went in.

"Well, if it isn't the girls' junior league basketball practice!" Bruce Patman, astride his bicycle and with his arms folded across his chest, was stopped at the end of the Wakefield driveway, a sneer on his lips.

He grinned suddenly. "Hey, Pee Wee, I guess you've got your game, huh? You've really met your match, now!" Delighted by his own joke, Bruce slapped his thighs, hopped back on the seat of his bicycle and rode down the street.

The smiles had immediately disappeared from Ken's and Elizabeth's faces. They stood like statues for a few seconds. Then, with an angry jerk of his shoulders, Ken turned around and ran down the driveway.

"Hey, watch it!" cried Jessica, who was just turning up toward the house. Ken had nearly run right into her.

Without an answer, Ken hurried on his way, leaving both of the Wakefield twins staring after him.

Five

◇

Jessica Wakefield turned to her sister with a frown. "What was that puny guy doing over here, anyway?"

The two girls were walking back up to the house. Elizabeth had promised to keep Ken's secret, so she didn't answer.

"You might think about me next time you invite some geeky guy over," Jessica continued. "What if Bruce Patman or somebody went by," she said, sounding horrified. "Not everyone can tell us apart, you know."

Elizabeth shrugged as they entered the house. "Well, as a matter of fact, Bruce Patman did ride by a little while ago, but I'm positive he knew it was me."

She didn't add, "And I think he's the meanest and most horrible person in the world." Instead, she decided to change the subject. "So what did you think of the tryouts, anyway? It was a pretty good turnout, don't you think?"

"If half the girls in our class is a good turnout." Jessica giggled. "I knew everyone would want to try out. But *please*! Most of them were so pathetic, Liz, I thought I would die."

Elizabeth punched her sister playfully on the arm. "You'll get over it."

Pausing on the steps, Jessica turned. "Do you think you'll be talking to Amy Sutton later?" she asked casually.

"Probably. Why?" A note of concern and crept into Elizabeth's voice.

"Well, it's just that . . ." Jessica toyed with the zipper of her jacket. "I hate to make people feel rejected. Maybe you could suggest she drop out," she finished in a rush. "Lizzie, she was so clumsy, in case you hadn't noticed."

Elizabeth's forehead creased with anxiety. "Yeah, I know," she said sadly. "I saw her."

When the phone rang later, Jessica raced to pick it up. But when she discovered that it was Amy Sutton on the other end, she dropped the phone like a hot potato. "*E-liz-abeth*! Pho-one," she cried before running back into her room and slamming the door.

Elizabeth picked up the phone and was immediately greeted by Amy's excited voice. Elizabeth tried to erase the memory of how hurt she had been when her friend ignored her earlier that day. "Hi, Amy. What's up?"

"Well, I just wanted to say I'm sorry for acting like such a jerk before." Amy's giggle came over the line. "I was so psyched out about the tryout. And that I've been practicing until this very minute." There was a pause. "Forgive me?"

Elizabeth chuckled. "That's okay, Amy. No problem." She paused before going on. "You're still planning to try out, then?"

"Sure, why not?"

"I—I don't know. I just wondered."

"Well nothing's changed, Elizabeth. Except maybe I want to be a Booster even more now than I did before." Amy sighed heavily over the phone. Then her voice changed, sounding almost too casual as she asked, "Say, was that Ken Matthews I saw you talking to in the gym?"

"Uh-huh. We were talking about—" Elizabeth broke off suddenly. She didn't want to give Ken's secret away. "I was just apologizing to him for tripping him with my bookbag. I left it right in the way, and he fell over it. That's all."

"Oh . . . That's all it was?"

A curious smile broke out on Elizabeth's face as she began to wonder about all of Amy's questions. "That's all it was, Amy. I've got to go. See you tomorrow, okay?"

"Okay, Elizabeth. Bye."

The following day, Ken Matthews stopped by Elizabeth's locker before homeroom. He looked like a different person from the one he had been the day before. He seemed happy, confident, and hopeful.

"You know, I practiced with a tennis ball all last night, Elizabeth. You were right. It really works."

Elizabeth shut her locker and turned to face him with a smile. "That's great, Ken. I'm really glad for you. So, are you still thinking about that 'stupid old team'?" she teased.

"Am I ever!" Ken laughed. "And I owe it all to you, Elizabeth. Thanks." He put out his hand.

Elizabeth took Ken's hand and shook it firmly. "Glad to be of service." She giggled.

"Well, if it isn't the two midget basketball players." It was Bruce Patman again. He was grinning at them with his usual mean smile. Ken quickly let go of Elizabeth's hand. "Looks like you two just can't stay away from each other, huh? What a pair of lovebirds!" He elbowed the ribs of the boy standing next to him, and broke out in a fit of laughter.

"Oh, grow up, Bruce." Elizabeth spat out angrily. "You have a bad habit of turning up just where you're least welcome, and you're not funny at all!"

Holding up his hands, Bruce pretended to be surprised. "Oh, I'm not trying to be funny, Elizabeth. It's just that you two make such a nice couple. That's all." He winked at his friend again, and then burst out laughing. The two strolled down the hall, still laughing.

"That guy makes me so mad." Ken slammed a locker with the palm of his hand and frowned angrily at Bruce's retreating figure.

"Hey! Hey, Ken, take it easy." Elizabeth was surprised that Ken would get so mad. "Don't let him get to you so much. I mean, who cares what a stupid jerk like him says, anyway?"

Ken turned back to her, a look of distress on his face. "Maybe you don't care, Elizabeth, but I do. You know that by lunchtime half the school will think we're engaged or something. Bruce has got a mouth as big as the Rose Bowl."

"Oh, come on, Ken. Bruce won't even bother. He can't stay interested in one subject long enough to spread a false rumor."

But Elizabeth was wrong. By the end of the day, she noticed many of her classmates nudging one another and nodding in her direction. No one dated in the sixth grade at Sweet Valley Middle School, and the idea of Elizabeth and Ken as a couple was met with shock. Some people thought it was the biggest joke of the year, while others thought it was just plain gross.

When Jessica heard about Ken and her twin she was frantic. How could Elizabeth put her in such an awkward position? Lila and the other Unicorns had been a little cold when the subject of Elizabeth and Ken came up at lunchtime. At the end of ballet practice that day, Jessica decided to set Elizabeth straight.

"Don't you realize what this sort of thing can do to me?" she said, pulling her twin to one end of the Dance Studio.

Elizabeth shook her head. "Jess, nothing's going on. Ken and I are just friends."

Jessica groaned. "That's what they all say!" She let out a deep breath and pushed her hair back. "Listen, just stay away from Ken, Lizzie. It's really bad for my reputation."

Her sister stared at her in surprise. "Jessica, the rumors are about me, not you."

"I know that, Elizabeth. If they were about me, I'd kill myself. But it's my twin sister that's going out with that midget, and that connects me, whether I like it or not. So for my sake if it's true, cut it out. And if it's not true, then for goodness' sake, Lizzie, tell everyone! Think of me for once."

Elizabeth clenched her teeth. It was ridiculous to her that everyone would believe such a dumb story on Bruce Patman's word. And furthermore, she refused to set anybody straight about it. She knew that everyone would only take that as further proof, just as Jessica did. Besides Elizabeth didn't care about the rumors anyway. As long as she and Ken knew they were just friends, it didn't matter what everyone else thought.

The next day, Elizabeth caught up with Amy after school. "Want to walk home together?" she asked breathlessly. She fell into step beside her friend.

"Where's Jessica?" Amy asked.

Elizabeth shrugged. "She's meeting with the Unicorns today at the Dairi Burger."

"Those Unicorns," Amy said with a lopsided grin. "They really are a pack of cats, aren't they?"

"Not Jessica!" Elizabeth retorted hotly. "She's not like the rest of them."

Amy shrugged her shoulders. "Sorry. It's just that—" She stopped suddenly, looking at the ground.

"What? What is it?" Elizabeth looked at her friend with a frown, then followed Amy's gaze. At their feet on the sidewalk was an arrow-pierced heart scrawled in red chalk. Inside were the initials "EW" and "KM."

Elizabeth made a little sound of disgust. "Oh, no. This is so dumb." She grinned at Amy. But her smile quickly disappeared when she saw the dismay on her friend's face.

"Amy! Listen, it's not true." Catching Amy's arm, Elizabeth looked into the other girl's eyes. "Ken and I are just friends. He came over to my house once, and suddenly we're Romeo and Juliet. It's just a rumor Bruce started for spite." She shook her head as if she couldn't believe it had gone so far. "You'd think the whole school had seen us making out in the back of Guido's, or something. It's so ridiculous."

A look of relief crossed Amy's face, followed quickly by one of anger. "That stupid Bruce Patman! Boy, if I get my hands on him, I'll knock his brains out." The tomboy in Amy had not completely disappeared when she'd started sixth grade.

Amy shook her head, then turned to Elizabeth. "But why didn't you try to deny it? Wouldn't that have stopped all the gossip?"

Elizabeth smudged the heart out with her foot. "Probably not. Besides, it doesn't matter what everyone else thinks. The important thing is I know the truth, and so does Ken." She grinned. "And so do you."

"Yeah. I saw that stupid heart, too," a voice behind them said.

Both girls turned to see Ken Matthews with a sheepish grin on his face.

"Kind of embarrassing, huh?" He shifted his book bag from one hand to the other. "So what are we going to do about it?"

"Nothing," said Elizabeth, as they started to walk again. "Absolutely nothing. People who spread gossip only wind up looking stupid in the end."

"Why does Bruce have it in for you so bad, anyway?" Amy asked Ken.

"He doesn't want me trying out for the basketball team," Ken replied, a slight blush coloring his features. "He thinks I'm too short."

"No you're not!" Amy protested.

"Well, I'm not going to let him scare me away," Ken said firmly. "I know I can do it."

"All right, Ken!" Elizabeth exclaimed.

"I think that's a really good attitude," Amy declared as the trio reached her corner. "You shouldn't let people talk you out of doing something you really want to do, just because they don't like you for some reason."

Elizabeth noticed that Ken gave Amy an admiring look.

"Anyway," Amy continued. "I've got to go. See you both tomorrow. And believe me, Ken, if I can put up with the Unicorns not wanting me on the Booster squad, you can put up with dumb old Bruce Patman."

Six

◇

Elizabeth was trying to concentrate on her article about the tryouts, but she couldn't hear herself think. The pulsing rhythms of Johnny Buck's latest album, *The Buck Stops Here*, came quite clearly through the wall of Jessica's room. With a sigh, Elizabeth closed her notebook and went next door.

"Jess, could you turn that down, please?"

Jessica was practicing cheering in front of the mirror as she sang along to the music. "What? Oh, yeah, go ahead," she said without turning around.

Elizabeth walked over to the stereo and smiled as she noticed a striped cap sitting on one of the speakers. Elizabeth picked it up slowly and turned it around in her hands. No one would have known from looking at it that it was Jessica's most treasured possession.

The last time Johnny Buck was in town for a concert, she and Jessica had joined the crowd outside his hotel in an attempt to get his autograph. Elizabeth was thrilled when Johnny had thrown his cap into the mob and she had caught it. But Jessica had insisted he had thrown it to her. After all, she argued, he was looking right at her when he threw it. Rather than argue, Elizabeth gave the cap to Jessica. She could see how much more important it was to her twin than to her.

Elizabeth shrugged and put down the cap. A gorgeous rock star's cap wasn't worth a fight with your twin sister. Besides, Jessica was crazy about him. The focal point of her pink-and-white room was a full-length poster of Johnny Buck. The mirror could hardly be seen under all the clipped-out magazine pictures and newspaper stories about him.

Jessica turned away from the mirror and kicked her right leg in front of her in a graceful leap. "Sorry it was so loud, but isn't that the most outrageous song Johnny's ever done?"

Her sister shrugged. "I don't know. It's pretty good, I guess."

"Pretty good!" Jessica ran to the poster of Johnny Buck and spread her hands over his ears. "Don't you listen to her! You're great! That's a *great* song!" She pointed an accusing finger at her twin, her dimpled smile playing about the corners of her mouth. "*You* need a lesson in taste!"

Elizabeth laughed. "Yeah, that's what everyone keeps telling me."

The smile quickly disappeared from Jessica's face. "Speaking of taste, Elizabeth . . ." She strode over and lifted the tone arm off the record. "Would you please stop hanging around with Ken? It's humiliating."

"What are you talking about?" Elizabeth laughed again. She refused to take the matter seriously.

Her sister whirled around to face her. "I *saw* you walking home from school with him today. You can't deny it."

"Jessica, I don't want to deny it. But don't worry, no one would think it was you. I was with Amy Sutton too, and everyone knows you aren't exactly fond of her."

Jessica closed her eyes. "That's not the point, Elizabeth."

Jessica squeezed one hand with the other. Why couldn't Elizabeth understand? It made her look so bad in the eyes of the Unicorns, her sister, going out with the shrimpiest guy in their class.

"Look," she said, using her sweetest voice. "If it isn't true, why don't you just tell everyone? Couldn't you do that for my sake? Please?"

For a moment, Elizabeth was softened by her sister's plea. She did understand, even though Jessica would never believe it. But Elizabeth had made up her mind that she would not defend herself against lies. She didn't need to prove anything to anybody.

She turned away. "Sorry, Jess. I can't do that."

"But why? Why can't you, Lizzie? I don't understand," Jessica said in anguish.

Elizabeth absently picked up the cap again and sat on Jessica's bed. She turned the cap over and over in her hands as she searched for the right words. It upset her to hurt Jessica. She would give anything to protect her. But she just wouldn't give in on the issue.

"Jess, remember when we were little and Steven broke that china vase?" She paused as Jessica nodded. "And Steven told Mom that I broke it, so Mom punished me." With a sigh, Elizabeth put the cap down and stood up. "And because I didn't say anything, Steven confessed," she continued. "Well, this is sort of like that time, Jessica. I really think it's wrong to tell lies and spread rumors. People who do always end up wishing they hadn't." Elizabeth walked toward the door. "I don't need to deny I'm friends with Ken," she declared. "But I'd bet anything that Bruce ends up wishing he'd kept his big mouth shut."

*   *   *

Ken sat on the edge of his bed with his elbows on his knees and tossed the tennis ball from one hand to the other. After a few moments, he stood up and began bouncing the ball on the hardwood floor where he had pulled the rug back.

Even as he concentrated on the bright-yellow ball, he was thinking over his conversation with Amy Sutton. "You shouldn't let people talk you out of doing something you really want to do," he repeated, remembering her words. Amy was right, and Ken knew it. If he wasn't good enough, then he wouldn't make the basketball team. But he would let the coach decide that, not Bruce Patman.

Ken grinned and shook his head. "You're all right, Amy," he said out loud, with a soft chuckle.

He returned his attention to the bouncing tennis ball. He'd been practicing for at least a couple of hours every night since Elizabeth had taught him the trick. There was no question in his mind that he had improved. He could feel it. Now he constantly kept his eyes on the ball and never tried to shoot or pass blindly, as he used to. It didn't matter that the ball was so much smaller than a basketball. He was confident that he could use the same concentration on the basketball court.

After a few moments, Ken raised his head and listened to the silence of his house. It was late afternoon, and a warm sunset glow came through his bedroom window. He was ready.

Ken headed down the stairs with a determined look on his face. He flicked on the light and made his way down the steps to his basement.

From a closet in the old playroom, he took his father's basketball. He bounced it experimentally on the cement floor, and the sound echoed cavernously off the hard walls. For a moment, Ken was paralyzed by the unexpected loudness. His nervousness returned briefly. But he drew a deep breath and started bouncing the basketball with the same rhythm he had developed with the tennis ball.

Slowly at first, and then with increasing speed and confidence, Ken dribbled the basketball around the basement. He ran in tight circles, passing the ball behind himself and through his legs. He backed up, keeping the ball only inches from the floor, and then surged forward, the ball bouncing up high to meet his hand.

He passed to himself, rebounding the ball off the cement walls of the playroom. And then, without hesitating for a moment, he shot the ball fifteen feet to the large wastebasket across the room. With a soft metallic scrape, the garbage can skidded backward. The ball had landed squarely inside.

"Score!" cried Ken, thrusting out two fingers for a count.

He stood grinning for a moment. Then he caught his breath and jogged slowly forward to pick up the ball.

"OK, Matthews. So you scored. Big deal. Now let's start practicing!"

"One, two, three, four," Amy whispered, kicking her left leg with the rhythm of her baton. "One, two, up, catch, twirl, twirl, three, four." She went steadily on, practicing the complicated maneuvers with enough strength and skill to make up for her lack of natural grace.

As the sun dipped below the horizon Amy continued her baton drills. She pushed her hair out of her eyes with an impatient hand. *Concentrate. Concentrate,* she told herself.

The flickering silver baton caught and reflected the last rays of the setting sun as it spun over Amy's head. She tossed it up and caught it with a flourish. "Not bad," she said, a grin highlighting her flushed face. "I'd say definite Booster material."

"Amy! Aren't you coming inside? It's getting dark." Mrs. Sutton's figure was silhouetted against the light pouring from the doorway.

"Yeah, Mom. Right now." Amy jogged into

the house from the backyard. She smiled as her mother put her arm around her.

"I don't think my sister had any idea what she was doing when she taught you how to twirl that baton," Mrs. Sutton teased. "She created a cheerleading monster."

"Well, first I've got to pass the tryouts. Then we'll see who's a cheerleader," Amy added with a smile. The phone rang as Amy reached for a can of soda. "I'll get it."

"Hello, Amy, is that you?" an unfamiliar voice came through the line.

"Yes, who's this?"

"It's Lila Fowler—"

"And Ellen," Ellen Riteman added, obviously speaking from an extension.

Amy put the soda down, a feeling of anger and anxiety starting to creep in. It wasn't likely that the two Unicorns were calling for pleasant chitchat.

"Listen, Amy," Lila began. "We really think you should drop out of the Booster tryouts. There are plenty of other girls better than you."

Amy's heart sank. Why would they call her to say this? "Do you mean you're making the cuts before the auditions?" she demanded, trying not to let her voice give away how nervous she was.

There was a pause on the other end before Ellen spoke in a coaxing voice. "No, of course not,

Amy. We just thought . . . you know. We just thought we'd save you the embarrassment of being rejected."

"Yeah," cut in Lila. "So why not just forget it, Amy? Don't waste your time getting your hopes up. I bet you have a lot of work to do for the class newspaper."

Amy swallowed. "Does Ms. Langberg know what you're doing?"

There was another pause. Then Lila spoke again. "No, of course she doesn't. This is just between us. We're only trying to do you a favor."

"What?" The word came out with a surprised laugh. Suddenly Amy felt in control. "Listen, you guys, I don't know what your idea of a favor is, but this sure isn't mine." She rushed on before the Unicorns could interrupt her. "And I am definitely not dropping out of the auditions. If you want to cut me after I audition, then go ahead. But you can't scare me away!"

Lila's voice came over the line. It was soft and slightly threatening. "Amy, you're making a big mistake. Drop out. I mean it."

"*No!*" Amy slammed the receiver down before Lila or Ellen could answer her. She stood for a moment by the phone, slightly out of breath and shivering. "No," she whispered, shaking her head. "No way."

Seven

◇

"Pizzaburgers again! I swear, we should go on a hunger strike." Jessica set her tray down at the Unicorns' lunch table and slid into a chair next to Lila.

"Hmm," said Lila. She munched a carrot stick and eyed Jessica's lunch suspiciously. "You shouldn't eat stuff like that anyway," she said, pulling another carrot stick from a plastic bag. "You'll get fat." Lila silently held out the bag.

Jessica blushed and looked down at her food, her appetite suddenly gone. Lila could do that sometimes. She laughed nervously and reached for a carrot stick. "I don't even want it, anyway," she decided, pushing the untouched pizzaburger away.

"Did Ellen tell you about us calling Amy last

night?" Lila's voice was low, and she leaned forward to put her elbows on the table.

"Yeah. I can't believe she actually hung up on you guys," Jessica said, shaking her head in amazement.

Lila smiled scornfully. "Don't worry. When Janet and Ellen get here, we'll figure out what to do about her."

"All right."

"Oh, by the way," Lila added casually, picking a tiny bit of fuzz off her sweater. "Guess who's coming to Sweet Valley?"

Jessica's blue-green eyes lit up with anticipation. "Who?" she asked breathlessly.

A huge smile broke out on Lila's face. "Johnny Buck."

"*No!*" Jessica was in shock. For a moment she sat still, paralyzed with joy. Then she gulped, suddenly on fire with impatience. "When do tickets go on sale? I have to go! How much are they? What am I going to wear?"

Lila nodded, smiling. "The tickets go on sale in a couple of days, I think. And they're twenty-five dollars."

"Each?" It seemed like an enormous sum to Jessica, especially considering she'd have to buy a new outfit and get all the concert paraphernalia. She glared at Lila briefly. Lila Fowler never worried about money. Her father was very wealthy, and wasn't around enough to know how she spent it, anyway.

Jessica's smile reappeared. No amount of money would be too much, she decided firmly. Suddenly, another thought occurred to her. "I just hope I can go," she said.

"Why wouldn't you be able to?" Lila asked, her eyes widening with surprise.

Jessica shrugged. "I don't know. You never know what parents will or will not let you do. Last time he was in town my parents thought I was too young. Can you believe it? But I'll find a way," she said fiercely. "I'd rather die than miss his concert."

"Something's got to be done."

Startled, Jessica looked up as Ellen and Janet sat down with them. She knew without asking what Janet meant, because she was glaring fiercely at Amy Sutton, who had walked in ahead of them. Having to deal with Amy drove away the excitement Jessica and Lila had felt over Johnny Buck's concert. Jessica knew she had to take a stand and prove to her friends that she was with them one-hundred percent. "About Amy?" she asked hesitantly.

Janet nodded, opening her own bag of raw vegetables. "Yeah," she said, taking a huge bite of celery. Through the crunching she added, "That girl just doesn't know when to quit. We've got to teach her a lesson, and we think we know how. You've got to help us, Jessica."

Jessica hesitated. What if their plan hurt Elizabeth, too? Elizabeth was friendly with Amy, and the Unicorns' plan might involve her. The idea made her very uncomfortable. Jessica had to be sure Elizabeth wouldn't be involved and that she would never find out what they were up to.

But whatever the plan was, Jessica was a Unicorn, and she knew she'd have to go along with what the other Unicorns wanted. She drew a deep breath. "Okay, what is it?"

Ellen and Lila exchanged a knowing look, and then both burst into giggles. Janet nodded. "We're going to send Amy some fan mail."

An expectant smile broke over Jessica's features. This was beginning to sound good. Suddenly all her determination returned. Elizabeth could take care of herself.

"Care to explain that?" she asked, helping herself to another carrot stick.

Ellen leaned forward. "Well," she said, her blue eyes sparkling, "We thought we'd just write a letter from Ken Matthews to Amy."

"No!" Jessica was scandalized—and delighted. Her mind began to race as she thought of all the possible consequences of the plan. First of all, it didn't affect Elizabeth at all. It was just between Amy and Ken.

With growing excitement, Jessica pulled out a spiral notebook, and opened it to a blank page. She raised one eyebrow. "So, where do we begin?"

"You do it, Jessica." Janet sat back, grinning.

Jessica smiled and bent over her notebook. Her pen flew quickly over the paper. "Now this! *This* will blow her mind."

> Dear Amy,
>   I watched you at cheerleading practice. I hate to say it, but the other girls are a lot better than you, and I think you should quit. I'm saying this because I really like you and I don't want you to get hurt. But no way are they going to pick you. When you're up against competition as awesome as the Unicorns, you shouldn't even bother. Even Elizabeth agrees with me.
>   Maybe we could sit together at lunch sometime.
>
>   From,
>   Ken

The Unicorns took turns reading the note and smiling with satisfaction. But another idea was forming in Jessica's mind. If she could make sure that Elizabeth, Amy, and Ken would stop being friends, she'd be even more delighted.

"How about one more?" she said slowly, as the plan unfolded itself. "Let's write a little love letter to Ken from Amy."

Ellen frowned. "I don't get it."

"I do," Lila cut in, her smile matching Jessica's. "It's a sort of insurance."

The rest of the Unicorns nodded as they figured out what Jessica wanted to do.

"How should it start?" asked Mary Giaccio, a seventh grader, licking her lips.

Lila smiled slyly. "Well, for starters, I think 'Dear Ken.'"

"No!" interrupted Janet, her eyes shining. "'My dearest Ken' would be better."

"Yeah," Mary cut in. "It's got to be gushy—so Ken will just die of embarrassment."

Lila nodded. "You're right. We'll fix it so he never talks to her or Elizabeth again."

Jessica chewed thoughtfully on the end of her pencil. A smile broke gradually over her face as an idea came to her. She looked at Lila with a triumphant gleam in her eye. "I've got it. Feast your eyes on this."

The Unicorns leaned across the table and looked over Jessica's shoulder as she started to write. Every now and then a giggle escaped from the group. The tip of Jessica's tongue showed between her lips, she was concentrating so hard. Finally she was done.

Dearest Ken,

    The past week has been terrible. Or do I mean wonderful. Ever since getting to know you, I can't stop thinking about you. Every time I see you walking down the hall, I wish we were walking together. I even dream about you. It's wonderful! I don't care if you're so much shorter than me. I love you anyway, Ken, I really do.

    I talked to Elizabeth about this and she told me I should come right out and tell you. She's always saying honesty is the best policy, and she's right. But I'm too shy to tell you to your face. So next time you see me, all you have to do is smile, and I'll know you feel the same way too. Oh Ken! I can't live another day without knowing if you love me, too!

    I love you.

Love and kisses,
Amy

Lila shook her head with appreciation. "Jessica, you have really outdone yourself this time. I guess Elizabeth isn't the only one in your family who can write." She looked down at the letter again. "I especially love the line about not caring if he's so much shorter. It's great."

"Yeah," said Ellen. "It's really a masterpiece. The whole thing."

"Ken will absolutely die," declared Mary.

Jessica looked up. "Well, that ought to do it. This will put an end to Elizabeth, Amy, and Ken hanging around together." Then she thought of something. "I can slip this one to Amy. But how should we give Ken his?"

Ellen smiled. "His locker is a few down from mine. I could slide it under the door." She adjusted a purple ribbon around her hair and read the letters once more. "Hey, Jessica. How come you put in these parts about Elizabeth?"

"That way Ken and Amy will both stay away from her, too," Jessica answered impatiently.

She smiled at her own cleverness. Ken and Amy would just stop being friendly toward Elizabeth. Her twin would never know why. There was no way Elizabeth would ever find out about these letters. After all, Ken and Amy wouldn't tell her, and none of the Unicorns were about to spoil their perfect plan!

Besides, she was sure Elizabeth wouldn't mind that much anyway. Jessica couldn't believe that Elizabeth really did want to be friends with those two. She figured Elizabeth was just nice to them out of pity. That was typical of her twin.

Lila tossed her light-brown hair back over her shoulder. With a sly smile, she said, "You think of everything, don't you?"

Jessica Wakefield grinned. She ripped Ken's

letter from the notebook and folded it carefully. Then she put his name on it and handed it across the table to Ellen.

"Do you think you can have it written by to-morrow afternoon?" Elizabeth asked Amy as they walked down the hall. "I'd like to put it in this week's *Sweet Valley Sixers*.

Amy shrugged. "Sure, I guess so. Oh, you know what?" she continued with a lopsided grin. "The Unicorns have struck again. At least I think it's them."

Elizabeth looked at her friend, a worried frown passing briefly across her face. "What did they do now?"

Amy stopped for a minute and shifted her books from one arm to the other. "I got this note," she explained, "that said it was from Ken, and it told me to quit the Booster tryouts. But I know Ken would never write that, especially after we had that talk about basketball and all that. Don't you think?" she looked hopefully into Elizabeth's eyes.

"Oh, Amy! How could they? I'm sure Ken wouldn't write something like that. The only logi-cal answer is that it's the Unicorns, still trying to scare you off." Elizabeth shook her head angrily.

"Yeah, that's what I figure. Hey, there's Ken. I can ask him. Hey, Ken, wait up!"

As Elizabeth and Amy hurried to meet Ken,

he turned and saw them. To their surprise, he slammed his locker shut and rushed away down the hall.

Amy stared at Elizabeth with an expression of disbelief. "What was that all about?"

"Beats me," Elizabeth answered, looking down the hallway after Ken. "I guess something must be bothering him. It can't be that dumb letter. Maybe it's Bruce again."

"Maybe," said Amy. She turned quickly to Elizabeth again. "Look, I'm going to go find him and see what's bugging him, OK? And just make sure about this letter. I'll see you later."

Elizabeth nodded. "Sure. 'Bye, Amy."

Within minutes, Amy had tracked Ken down outside the library. She was out of breath from running, and had to grab his arm to get his attention.

When Ken saw who it was, he turned bright red and pulled his arm away. He began backing up and stumbled over his shoelace. He fell over backward, his books flying in all directions.

Amy bent down quickly to help him up.

"Don't bother. I can get them," Ken mumbled. He avoided looking at her, but Amy could see his forehead was creased with an angry scowl.

"Hey, Ken. What's wrong?" Amy dropped the books she had picked up, feeling hurt and confused.

Ken's face flushed even darker, and he awkwardly scrambled to his feet. He started to back away. "Nothing. I—I've got to go." He turned and ran, not looking back even once.

Amy stood there, her own face flushed, too. What was Ken upset about? Was he mad at her? She started walking back down the hallway, trying to figure out what she could have done to make him mad. Maybe he thought she'd dropped out of the Booster tryouts. Maybe he'd heard about the Unicorns trying to scare her off. Maybe he thought they had succeeded.

There's no way, Ken, Amy said to herself. *No way will I drop out. Especially not now. I'll show them I'm not scared.*

Meanwhile, Ken hurried down the hall, feeling angry and embarrassed. Why did Amy have to go and spoil everything by writing that stupid letter?

"Girls," he muttered, his face crimson. Just when you started to be friends with them, they turned all mushy on you. But Amy? He never would have expected it of her. That was why he'd liked her in the first place. Now he could never face her again.

"Did you do it?"

Ellen looked in the mirror. The long row of bathroom stalls was reflected behind her. She took out a hairbrush and started brushing her glossy dark curls before she answered Lila. "Uh-huh. Special delivery."

Lila leaned forward over the sink and examined her face. When she spoke she didn't bother to lower her voice. "Good. Serves Amy right, you know. This'll teach her for being so stubborn. I don't know why she ever thought she could try out for Boosters."

"Absolutely," Ellen agreed. "All I can say is she asked for it." She giggled. "Wouldn't you have loved to see the look on Ken's face when he read that love letter?"

With one hand on her heart, Lila leaned back over the sink in a dramatic pose. "Oh, Ken!" she gasped. "I can't live another day without knowing if you love me, too."

Ellen took another melodramatic pose, falling to one knee before Lila. "Every time I see you walking down the hall I wish we were walking together!" The two cousins collapsed into giggles. "Jessica is a true poet," declared Lila. "I've got to hand it to her. That letter was perfect."

"Well, she had a good reason for wanting to get Ken," Ellen said, crossing her arms. "I would be completely humiliated if a sister of mine was hanging around with such a dork."

The bathroom door opened and another girl came in. She looked timidly at the two Unicorns.

Lila gave the girl a look that clearly said "Hurry up."

When the two girls were alone again, Ellen took a final look in the mirror. "Well, you can be sure Ken will stay pretty far away from Elizabeth and Amy now. He'll be so embarrassed he won't even show up for basketball tryouts." She smiled slyly at Lila. "We've fixed Amy and Ken for good."

Lila Fowler smoothed the denim skirt she was wearing and gave her reflection a critical glance. "Not quite," she said slowly.

Ellen looked at her sharply. "What's that supposed to mean?" she asked.

"I mean we're not done with Amy yet," Lila said firmly. "The final auditions are today, and if she's still stubborn enough to show up, we're going to have a little surprise for her."

Ellen stared at Lila for a moment, waiting for her to explain further. She grew impatient. "What are we going to do?"

With a toss of her head, Lila turned away. "Not until the auditions. Then I'll tell everyone at once." She waited to see if Ellen would object. After a moment, she turned back to face her. "Let's go."

The two Unicorns walked out of the girls' room into the bustling hallway of Sweet Valley Middle School.

At the far end of the lavatory, the door of the

last stall opened. Elizabeth Wakefield walked out, trying to control her trembling. She had never been so angry in her life. It was Jessica who had written that letter to Amy! But it seemed that wasn't the only letter.

Elizabeth would take care of her twin later. For now, the important thing was to find Amy and stop her from going to the auditions before something terrible happened.

Eight

◇

Elizabeth hurried down the empty corridor, anxiously checking her watch. The last class of the day had ended before she'd gone into the lavatory, and after-school activities didn't start for another fifteen minutes. She had to find Amy.

Elizabeth was terribly worried about her friend. If she went to the Booster auditions, there was no telling what Lila would do to her.

Lost in thought, Elizabeth rounded a corner and ran smack into Ken.

"Oh, sorry," he mumbled, dodging away from her.

"Ken! Ken, wait!"

Elizabeth chased after him. She couldn't let him go on thinking Amy had written that love letter.

She caught up with him. "Now listen to me, Ken. I'm not letting you go until you hear what I'm going to tell you." Elizabeth looked straight into his eyes, her forehead creased.

Ken gulped. "Wha—what is it?" He was blushing bright red, and kept looking away, as if searching for a way to escape.

"Did you get some kind of letter from Amy Sutton?" Elizabeth asked.

The color of Ken's face deepened. "Listen, I don't want to talk about it, OK? Just forget it."

But Elizabeth wouldn't give up. "Well, did you?"

Ken met her worried gaze, his own eyes filled with embarrassment. He nodded at last.

Elizabeth leaned back against the wall. "Amy didn't write it, you know."

"Oh, come on, Elizabeth. You don't have to cover up for her." He sighed heavily. "I just don't want to talk about her. It doesn't matter anyway."

"But it does!" Elizabeth straightened up. "Amy is your friend. She's a good person to have as a friend." She looked frantically into his face. She hoped she would see something that told her he understood.

"Ken, let me see the letter. Please?"

Ken stared at her, a shocked expression on his face. "Are you kidding me?" He looked embarrassed again. "Besides, what makes you so sure I didn't throw it away?"

Elizabeth shrugged. "I was just hoping you didn't. Did you?"

With a sigh, Ken dug into his pocket. He pulled out the crumpled note and handed it to Elizabeth without a word.

She took the letter and read it quickly.

"Did you ever see Amy's handwriting?" she asked when she had finished.

Ken shrugged. "No."

"Well, I have. And it isn't like this." It was her turn to look embarrassed. "But I do know whose handwriting this is."

"Well?" Ken looked at her expectantly.

Elizabeth's mouth was set in a stern line. "It's my sister's."

Confusion spread over Ken's face. "What? I don't . . ." His voice trailed off.

"You see," Elizabeth began, "Jessica and the Unicorns think they can make people do anything they want. Like they didn't want you and me to be friends, and they didn't want you and Amy to be friends. And they don't want Amy trying out for Boosters."

Ken shook his head. "I still don't get it. So why did Jessica write this letter and sign Amy's name?"

"Because. They knew you'd get really angry

when you read it and never talk to Amy again. Or me, either." Elizabeth shook her head sadly.

Ken let out a low whistle. "You mean they hate her so much they just want to hurt her? Like this?"

"I don't know." A puzzled frown creased Elizabeth's forehead. "They even wrote her a fake note from you. I'm not sure they really hate her. They just don't want her trying out for the Boosters. They don't think she's pretty enough, or something, so they wanted to hurt her enough to make her quit." She gave an angry shake of her head. "I don't know. It's just so stupid and mean." There was silence for a moment. Elizabeth bit her lip and looked at Ken.

"I'm really sorry, Ken."

"What for? You didn't write it."

Elizabeth nodded. "I know, but Jessica did. So I feel partly to blame for it. That's one of the consequences of being a twin."

The two started walking down the hallway toward the gym. "Look," Ken continued. "Just because you two are identical twins doesn't mean you're the same person. Let's just forget it, OK?"

They walked for a moment in silence, then Ken chuckled. "You know, I really couldn't believe Amy would write it anyway."

"Well, of course not!" Elizabeth laughed, tossing her golden ponytail. "Amy would never do something like that. She knew you couldn't have written the one she got."

With a shrug of his shoulders, Ken gave Elizabeth a sheepish grin. "Well, I guess I'd better straighten it out with her. After the way I've been acting, she must think I'm crazy."

Elizabeth stopped suddenly and her hand flew to her mouth. "Oh, no! I've got to find her. It's almost time for the Booster tryouts! Come on, you've got to get to the locker room and change."

"Uh, yeah," Ken mumbled, suddenly feeling nervous.

As they arrived at the gymnasium, Elizabeth wished a hurried "good luck" to Ken and raced inside. She glanced around the huge room for her friend. She soon spotted Amy on the floor and strode over to where she was warming up. "Amy, I've got to talk to you," Elizabeth said in a whisper.

Amy saw the serious look on Elizabeth's face and quickly stopped. "What's wrong?"

Elizabeth came straight to the point. "I overheard Lila and Ellen in the girls' room. The Unicorns wrote that letter to you. They also wrote a love letter to Ken and signed your name."

"What!" Amy stared openmouthed at Elizabeth. She shook her head slowly. "Ken . . ." she said, an angry frown pulling her brows together. "No wonder."

Elizabeth stood silently watching her friend. She had just told on Jessica, and she felt terrible. But Jessica had hurt two people who hadn't done anything wrong. And even if she felt like a traitor, Elizabeth couldn't let her sister spoil her friendship with Amy.

Amy sniffed and looked over at the Unicorns. Trying to control her emotions, she pressed her lips together and drew a deep breath. "I can't believe it. No, I *can* believe it." She turned back to Elizabeth, her voice bitter. "Do you know what they did last night?"

"All I know is they called you," Elizabeth answered. "But what did they say?"

Amy gave a short laugh. "They told me that I should drop out of the tryouts, because they didn't want to see me get hurt," she said with heavy sarcasm. "They said they wanted to keep me from being rejected, so they were doing me a favor. The same stuff Ken supposedly wrote."

"Well, what did you say?" Elizabeth asked.

Amy shrugged. "What else? I said they couldn't scare me off like that. If they wanted to cut me after the audition, fine, but there was no way I was going to quit just because they wanted me to." She shook her head again, as if she still couldn't believe what they had done. "It really burns me up that they think they can scare me away that easily."

Elizabeth shook her head, too. "Well, from what I could tell from their conversation, one of the reasons they wrote that letter was to get back at you for not dropping out. 'Being stubborn,' they called it." She paused, looking at her friend. "I'm sorry, Amy."

Walking slowly to the bleachers, Amy smiled for the first time. "Hey, maybe some people can't tell you and Jessica apart, but I can. You don't have to apologize."

"Thanks." Elizabeth joined her on the bottom step of the bleachers. She sighed. ".Well, I guess they won, though, after all."

Amy stared at her in surprise. "What are you talking about?"

A blush warmed Elizabeth's face as she stammered, "But you've got to quit now, Amy."

"No, I do not."

Elizabeth's face grew hot as she tried desperately to save her friend from embarrassment. "But, Amy, they would rather die than let you on the team now. And even if they did, how could you want to hang around with girls who did this to you?"

"Elizabeth, I've told you I don't want to be a Unicorn. I don't want to be friendly with them. I don't want to hang out with them. I just want to be a cheerleader." Amy's voice was low and intense. She clenched her fists with pent-up emotion.

An uncomfortable silence increased the tension between the two girls. Elizabeth didn't know what to say. All she knew was that the Unicorns were going to do something terrible to Amy if she couldn't convince her friend to pull out of the auditions.

Amy looked across the gym to where the other girls were warming up. "Elizabeth, I'm really surprised at you. After all that talk with Ken about doing what you want no matter how many people are against you. Doesn't that apply to me, too?" She looked at Elizabeth accusingly.

"Anyway," Amy continued. "It just wouldn't be right if I let them win. Even if I didn't want to be a cheerleader anymore, I'd go through with the audition just to keep them from getting their way. Somebody's got to stand up to them."

She stood up. "So. Are you going to watch?" she asked, not looking at Elizabeth.

"Amy, don't!" Elizabeth grabbed Amy's arm. "Don't you see? They aren't going to let you just audition and walk away. They're going to do something to you."

"Like what?" Amy laughed unsteadily. "They can't murder me in front of the whole gym, you know."

Elizabeth shook her head sadly. Her turquoise eyes were filled with worry. But Amy's words had stung her. Didn't the things she had said to Ken apply to Amy, too? Had she been guilty of encouraging him to do what she wanted Amy to give up on? She just wished there were some way to convince Amy that she'd be better off quitting.

"I don't know what they're planning. Lila wouldn't tell Ellen until they got here. But, Amy! Lila said they were really going to fix you." She looked frantically to either side of the gym. The bleachers were filling up with students waiting for the Booster auditions and the basketball tryouts. "And whatever it is, it's going to be in front of practically the whole school."

Amy looked around uneasily. By nature she was a shy girl, and she had come this far only because she wanted so much to be a cheerleader. The possibility of being set up by the Unicorns in front of so many people almost made her give in.

But she caught sight of Lila Fowler at the other end of the gym. And thinking of Lila's voice telling her they wanted to do her "a favor" made Amy mad enough to be brave.

She faced Elizabeth. "You're probably right," she said, nervously pulling at her limp hair. "But I don't care." Her voice strengthened. "I think I'm good enough so that they'll have to accept me whether they want to or not. Ms. Langberg will be watching, too, so they can't cut me if I'm really good."

Elizabeth sighed. She knew that Amy was right to stick up for herself. And she admired the way her friend was ready to face the Unicorns.

"I just hope you're right," she said finally. She looked into Amy's blue eyes. Suddenly she smiled. "Well, good luck."

Amy grinned back. "Thanks, Elizabeth. I think I'll need it."

Nine

Ken braced himself as he pushed open the locker-room door. He expected to hear at least one person yell "midget" at him when he walked in. But the other boys were too busy getting ready. Nobody seemed even to notice him.

He walked to his locker and sat down on the bench. Even though he knew he was a lot better than he had been the week before, he was nervous. And for some reason, he couldn't open his gym bag. He just sat looking at the other guys, thinking how tall they all were and how short he was.

The longer he sat, the harder it was for him to change into his gym clothes. In his imagination he saw his dad playing basketball with crowds cheering him. Finally, with an angry cry, he grabbed his bag and ran out of the locker room. And for the second time that day, he ran right into Elizabeth Wakefield, who was leaning over the water fountain for a drink.

"Ken! What's going on?" She quickly took in his angry scowl and his unpacked gym bag. Her eyes widened in alarm. "You're not leaving, are you?"

"Let's just forget it, Elizabeth, OK?" Ken turned away, his fists clenched. His face was an angry red.

Elizabeth moved around so she was in front of him, and made him look at her. "What happened? Did someone bother you again?" She shook her head. "I thought you'd decided you didn't care about that anymore."

"No." Ken sighed wearily. "But I know that as soon as I got out there on the court, Bruce would—" He broke off, struggling to explain. "I just couldn't take it, Elizabeth!"

"Oh, come on!" Elizabeth cut in angrily. "How long are you going to let him get in your way?"

Ken just looked at her, too ashamed and disappointed in himself to speak.

Elizabeth decided to use a different approach. "Listen, Ken," she continued in a softer tone. "You know what Amy said when I told her about that letter you got?"

He shook his head silently.

"I expected her to drop out of the auditions because she wouldn't have to have anything to do with the Boosters. But you know what she said?"

Ken shook his head again. "No. What?"

"She said that she'd go through with it now even if she didn't want to be a cheerleader." Elizabeth nodded when she saw how surprised and impressed Ken was. "Just so she could keep Lila Fowler and those Unicorns from getting their way."

Ken stared at her, his expression a mixture of astonishment and admiration. "She said that?" he wondered aloud.

"Yeah," Elizabeth replied, folding her arms triumphantly. "Now are you going to let Amy go through her auditions, and chicken out yourself?"

A hot blush colored Ken's features again. He lifted his chin, a new expression on his face. "No," he said. "I'll do it. I'll do it for Amy."

Elizabeth breathed a sigh of relief. "That's great, Ken. Good luck." She waited and watched until he had gone back into the locker room. Then she returned to the gym.

The Boosters were just starting to get under way as Elizabeth found a seat on the bleachers. There were about twenty-five girls present, a lot fewer than had come to the first audition, and many of them were already turning in their batons. Elizabeth guessed baton-twirling was really harder than it looked.

Within minutes, there were only Unicorns, friends of Unicorns, and Amy Sutton left at the tryouts. Elizabeth wondered if the Boosters had made any other phone calls, successful ones. Maybe that was why there weren't any "undesirables" left except Amy.

Lila stepped forward to make an announcement. "OK, this is what we're going to do next. All of you line up and hold out your batons. Then follow Ellen. She's going to do some basic stuff. If you mess up, you're out."

A ripple of surprise went through the girls and the crowd of people watching them. It was a harsh test, Elizabeth thought.

She glanced over to where Ms. Langberg was standing to oversee the auditions. The gym teacher looked a little surprised, but she didn't say anything. Elizabeth watched Lila again.

Lila nodded. "Go ahead, Ellen."

Looking very self-conscious, Ellen began going through the simpler baton drills. Most of the girls could follow, but as the twirling became more complicated, batons started dropping.

Amy bit her lip in concentration, forcing herself to be calm. She couldn't let the baton drop. She just couldn't. She avoided looking at any of the other girls in case she lost her nerve.

Keep your elbows relaxed, she said to herself. *Keep your eye on the baton. Stand up straight.*

Elizabeth's attention was focused on Amy. She knew there were spots for four more girls on the Boosters, to bring the total to eight. But judging from the competition, it looked as though Amy didn't stand a chance.

After all, four of the girls left were good friends of at least one Unicorn, and two of them were Unicorns. Elizabeth sighed. *Poor Amy,* she thought. *She'll be so disappointed.* Suddenly a noise made her look toward the other end of the gym.

Boys had started coming out of the locker room. And from the shouts and whoops of laughter, Elizabeth could tell they were all in high spirits for the tryouts. She quickly scanned the crowd of fast-moving boys, looking for Ken. There was no sign of him yet.

Bruce Patman was easy to spot, though. He always seemed to want more attention than anybody else. At that moment he was making a big deal out of shooting from the foul line. But Coach Cassels took charge just then.

"*Okay, gents*! Let's start some lay-ups for practice! Let's go! Let's go!" The coach's voice boomed out into the vast room.

Ellen paused briefly as she led the girls through the drills. She exchanged a look of frustration with the other Boosters. It made them angry to have to share the crowd's attention.

And the noise seemed to be having a bad effect on some of the girls trying out. In rapid succession, three girls lost their concentration and dropped their batons. With unhappy frowns, they stepped out of line and sat down.

Amy forced herself to be deaf to the loud distractions on the other side of the gym. "Just keep going," she said to herself. "Don't look at them."

When Ellen was done, there were only seven girls left, including Amy. Jessica, Lila, and Ellen were standing to one side. They had been watching Amy very carefully, and they were angry and worried because she hadn't messed up yet.

"What do we do if she's good?" whispered Ellen. She nodded in Amy's direction.

Jessica rubbed her palms on her tights, wondering the same thing. "She won't be. Don't worry," she whispered back. "She's the biggest klutzoid in California." But Jessica wasn't as confident as she looked. Amy wasn't being so klutzy after all.

"Well, she'll definitely spaz out when it's her turn to solo," she said under her breath. It was practically guaranteed.

The three girls suddenly realized that Ellen and the others were looking their way, waiting for the next step. Lila squared her shoulders and walked forward again.

"All right. Now for those of you still left, you're each going to have a chance to do a cheer with us Boosters, and then we'll lead right into the baton routine." She looked at the girls with a warm smile on her face. The smile faded when her eyes rested on Amy, but she soon pulled herself together.

She turned quickly to Ms. Langberg. "Do you think that's a good way to do it, Ms. Langberg?" she asked. She didn't want to take any chances, so she was pretending that they were letting their gym teacher have the final say on the auditions.

"Fine, Lila," Ms. Langberg said. "Go ahead."

Lila smiled sweetly at her, and then turned back to the girls. "We're going to do the same one we practiced last week, right? The 'He's our man' cheer. OK? Everybody remember it?"

The seven girls nodded.

"And remember if you drop your baton, you're *out*," put in Janet, looking straight at Amy.

"Penny," Lila said, pointing to the girl standing closest to her, "Why don't you go first?"

The pretty, fair-haired girl smiled and stepped out of line. The Boosters paired off on either side of her and gave her encouraging nods.

"Ready?" asked Jessica with a friendly smile. "Let's use—Oh, how about Dave?"

Penny giggled. Dave was the name of the boy she liked, and Jessica knew it. "Sure," she answered, still smiling.

At Jessica's signal, the five girls began the cheer, chanting "Dave, Dave, *he's* our man! If *he* can't do it no one can!" Five bodies moved in unison, and five strong voices sounded out together. When the cheer was over, the girls started the baton routine.

Elizabeth could tell that none of the Boosters were especially good with the baton, but at least no one dropped it. No one except Penny. As they tossed the batons up in front of them, Penny's slipped from her hand with a noisy clatter. It quickly rolled away on the floor.

There was a brief silence. Everyone looked at Penny in surprise. Her face held an expression of shock.

"Ohhh," she wailed. She covered her face with her hands and ran sobbing from the gym.

Elizabeth's heart went out to the girl. *She must have really wanted to join the Boosters*, she said to herself. The thought reminded her of Ken, and she quickly looked over to see if he had come out yet. For a moment, she was afraid he had left after all. Then she saw him. He was standing by himself, to one side, slowly dribbling a basketball.

As she was watching him, Ken looked up. He nodded, and Elizabeth breathed a sigh of relief.

"Wellll," Lila said after Penny disappeared. She shrugged. "OK, who's next? Grace?"

Another friend of the Unicorns walked up to the Boosters, and they settled on a name to use. The cheer was repeated, and the girls began the baton-twirling. True to her name, Grace finished without any mistakes.

There was scattered applause from the crowd in the bleachers. Grace blushed, and Lila patted her on the shoulder. "That was perfect, Grace."

The applause attracted the attention of the basketball players. Some of them stopped to watch the cheerleading tryouts.

Amy shifted from one foot to the other. She was nervous as she watched the girls perform. *I can do it*, she told herself every ten seconds. *I can do that*.

One by one, the other girls did the cheer with Jessica, Lila, Janet, and Ellen. No one else dropped the baton, but some were definitely better than others. Amy pulled nervously at her hair. Waiting to go last always made her tense. She just wanted to hurry up and get it over with.

And she hadn't forgotten Elizabeth's warning, either. She repeated her own words to herself. *They can't murder me in front of the whole gym.* But knowing the Unicorns they might come close.

"Amy!"

She jumped, startled from her thoughts. The

four Boosters were looking at her impatiently. It was her turn.

She came forward, and stood between Jessica and Ellen. Lila and Janet were at the ends. "I'm ready," Amy said, forcing her voice to sound sure and confident.

Jessica nodded and glanced quickly at Lila, who was standing next to her.

Lila nodded, too, and tried to keep a grin from coming to her lips.

"All right, Amy," Jessica said with an innocent smile. "Now, you know what to do. We'll all do the cheer with you, so you don't have to feel shy or anything."

Amy's lips were dry, and she licked them nervously. "Sure, no problem."

"OK, men! Stop gawking at the ladies and line up! Count off by twos!" Coach Cassels yelled to the boys who were just standing and watching. They ran to join the line.

"Now," continued Jessica. She was glad, for a change, for the noise at the other end of the gym. Maybe it would make Amy just nervous enough to drop her baton. "Let's take a name we haven't used yet. Any suggestions?" she asked, looking straight at Ellen.

Ellen pretended to be thinking. "I know!" she exclaimed with a smile. "How about Ken?"

Amy's heart jumped. The Unicorns really

knew how to play dirty. She knew this was going to be embarrassing. The bleachers were packed. But after all, she reasoned, it wasn't as if she would be doing it alone!

Ten

◇

"Get moving, Matthews!" Coach Cassels gave Ken an encouraging nod.

Ken nodded in response and joined the line of boys running to the basket for lay-ups. He waited nervously for his turn, staring at the hoop. He didn't want to meet the stares of any of the other boys. He wasn't going to give them a chance to tease him.

When his turn came, he bounced his ball a few times and then ran in. With a burst of speed, he jumped up, and bounced the ball off the backboard. It fell cleanly into the basket.

"Lucky break, midget!" jeered Bruce Patman. "Let's see you do it again!"

Ken glared at Bruce and took a place at the

end of the line. *Just you wait, Bruce,* Ken said to himself. *Just you wait.*

The next few minutes were spent on lay-ups. Ken missed a few, but he made more baskets than he lost. He still kept his head down and didn't look at any of the guys. He didn't want to see them laughing at him. He was afraid he'd lose his nerve if he did.

When the coach asked the boys to count off by twos, they lined up and did so quickly. Coach Cassels blew his whistle shrilly and announced a practice game, ones against twos.

Ken was a one, and he was pleased that Bruce Patman was a two. *I'll get you, Bruce. Just watch me.* Ken stood to one side, dribbling his ball.

Just then Ken looked over at the other side of the gym. He stopped bouncing the basketball for a moment. He could see Amy standing between Ellen Riteman and Jessica Wakefield.

"All right, now, on four," Jessica was saying. "One."

"Two."

The muscles of her right leg tensed as she prepared to kick.

"Three."

Amy's lips parted, and she drew a deep breath. *This is it. Let me be good,* she prayed.

"Four."

"Ken, Ken, he's our man!" Amy yelled at the top of her lungs as she kicked forward.

But she was cheering alone! Just as she had begun, the four Boosters had stepped backward, leaving her to scream by herself in the middle of the gym.

In less time than it took to think it all through, Amy decided to go ahead and finish.

"If he can't do it no one can!"

Elizabeth was horrified. So that was what the Unicorns had planned. They wanted to embarrass Amy by making her cheer all by herself!

Amy's voice rang out loudly across the gym. Just as he was dribbling toward the basket, Bruce Patman turned to see who was yelling.

The sight of Amy Sutton, all by herself, kicking and yelling her way through a cheer for that midget, Ken Matthews, was more than Bruce could stand. He stopped in his tracks and started laughing and pointing.

That was all the opportunity Ken needed. He ducked in toward Bruce and grabbed the basketball. He ran madly for the other end of the court. Bruce was left staring after him with a dumbstruck look on his face.

Weaving and turning, Ken dribbled the basketball with skill and coordination. The other players on his side took a moment to come to their senses. But then they ran with him, and they passed the ball back and forth on the way to the net.

Amy took it all in. Then, with even more energy than before, she started the cheer again. "Ken, Ken, he's our man! If he can't do it, no one can!"

The crowd quickly realized what was happening at the other end of the gym and started cheering. Ken Matthews was dodging around Bruce Patman, who had finally caught up. Ken's short size seemed to help him. He kept ducking and slipping around the other players. It seemed as if every time the opposite side thought they had the ball, Ken was running with it again. No one could catch him!

Coach Cassels was standing with his mouth open. His clipboard hung forgotten at his side. Was that *Matthews*?

Ken passed the ball between his legs and quickly spotted an opening behind Bruce. He jumped up for a basket—and in it went.

The kids in the stands went wild. It wasn't every day they got to see Bruce Patman left in the dust!

But their attention soon turned back to Amy. They couldn't believe what they were seeing.

After she had finished the cheer, Amy had started in on the Boosters' baton routine. But she didn't stop there. She was going off on her own routine now, the one she had been practicing for so long.

The baton flashed and spun as she twirled it over her shoulders and behind her back. It flipped under her legs, and flew higher and higher in the air as Amy spun beneath it. She grabbed the baton with her left hand as she was spinning it with her right, and passed it back. She didn't break the rhythm once.

The silver wand became hypnotic in Amy's hands. It spun faster and faster, and seemed to be everywhere at once. Amy's face was flushed with excitement and concentration. She looked like a different person.

Elizabeth stared at her, amazed. She knew Amy had been practicing, but this was incredible! No one could do what Amy was doing! She glanced quickly at the Boosters.

Jessica and the others were standing with their mouths hanging open, shocked. Jessica gulped and turned glazed eyes toward Lila. Lila just shook her head, speechless.

On the basketball court, Ken was aware that Amy was bringing down the house. It made him feel even more confident.

He looked for an opportunity and stole the ball again, dribbling like crazy for his team's hoop. He jumped and scored!

With a final flourish, Amy caught her baton and bowed low to the crowd.

No one knew whom to cheer for more—Amy Sutton or Ken Matthews. Everyone jumped up, screaming with excitement. Ken was quickly surrounded by his fellow basketball players. And Amy found herself being congratulated from all sides by the girls in the audition.

Through the crowd, Amy and Ken caught sight of each other. They both grinned. "We showed them, Amy!" yelled Ken.

She waved her baton, a tremendous smile threatening to split her face. "Boy, we sure did!" she cried.

After the crowd had disappeared, there were just a few people left in the gym. Amy was sitting on the bottom step of the bleachers next to Elizabeth, trying to catch her breath. She was exhausted. Never before had she been the center of attention like that.

She looked up as Jessica, Lila, Ellen, and Janet walked toward her. Amy cast a quick glance at Elizabeth and raised her eyebrows.

"Uh, Amy . . ." Jessica began, a blush turning her face pink. "We—" She turned to Lila and the others and then back to Amy, clearly embarrassed.

Amy tried not to smile. "Yeah? Did I make the squad?"

"Did you—" Jessica suddenly burst out laughing. It seemed to settle the tension. For the first time she spoke to Amy without being scornful. "You were great, Amy. That was outrageous."

Lila smiled weakly. "Yeah, we'd like you to be on Boosters, Amy. That is, if you want to," she added quickly.

"I want to," Amy answered, nodding her head. "And that's all I ever wanted, you know." She looked straight into Lila's eyes. Then she looked directly at each of the Boosters in turn. She shrugged. "Just let me know when practices are, that's all."

"Sure," said Jessica, smiling. She turned to the Unicorns. "Well, I guess we should figure out who else made the team, huh?"

Lila nodded, and the four moved away for a conference.

"Well, I guess I should say I'm sorry, Amy." Elizabeth looked at her friend with admiration and shook her head. "I shouldn't have been so down on you for trying out. I didn't exactly show a lot of confidence in you."

Amy smiled. "That's OK. I always knew you were just trying to get me to quit because you didn't want me to get hurt."

The two were silent for a moment. Slowly a grin stole over Amy's face. Elizabeth grinned back. Soon Amy was laughing.

"I almost died when I had to do that cheer all by myself!"

By then, Elizabeth was chuckling, too. "Well it's a good thing you didn't, or you wouldn't have gotten to see the Unicorns beg you to join the Boosters!"

Amy glanced over to the door of the boys' locker room. "Hey, there's Ken!"

Ken caught sight of them and came jogging over. He had just showered and changed, and he looked happy and relaxed.

"Whew!" he exclaimed, sitting down between the two girls. "This has been some day!"

"Listen, did you make the team?" Amy asked. "Am I going to get to cheer for you again?" Her eyes were sparkling.

Ken laughed. "Did I? The coach told me when we got inside the locker room that he was really proud that I'd be carrying on 'the Matthews tradition' at Sweet Valley." He chuckled again, but was suddenly serious. "I don't know how to tell my dad," he admitted with a nervous smile.

"Why?" Amy's voice rose. "He'll be so happy, Ken!" She looked at him, and a thought occurred to her. "Does he even know you were trying out?"

Ken covered his eyes with one hand and shook his head as though he were ashamed of himself. But the next moment he was peeking through his fingers and grinning at the two girls. "No! It's a surprise!"

Amy and Elizabeth laughed with him, and Elizabeth stood up. "Come on, you two winners," she teased. "Let's all go to my house and make celebration milkshakes. What do you say?"

Amy and Ken stood up too. The three of them looked at one another for a moment. Then they all burst into laughter.

Ken nodded. "Come on. Let's go!"

"Hey, by the way," Amy said suddenly about halfway to the Wakefields' home. "You know, I heard Johnny Buck is coming to Sweet Valley. Are you going to go?"

Elizabeth was surprised, and immediately thought of Jessica. In her imagination, she saw the striped cap sitting on Jessica's record collection. She saw the life-size picture of the handsome singer on the wall of Jessica's pink-and-white room, and the clippings crowded around the edges of the mirror. Elizabeth wondered if her sister knew that the man of her dreams was about to come to Sweet Valley.

She sighed. "I don't know. I guess I'd like to. But the last time he was here, my parents said we couldn't go." She grinned. "But we did go to his hotel, and we got his cap."

Amy shook her head with good-natured envy. Everyone in their school knew about Johnny

Buck's hat. "Boy, I'd even miss his concert to get a hat," she said.

Elizabeth chuckled. "Well I don't think Jessica would! This time she won't settle for just a hat," she added, suddenly serious. "If I know my sister, she'll do anything to go to that concert!"

Will Jessica find a way to attend Johnny Buck's concert? Find out in Sweet Valley Twins #5, Sneaking Out.